BY JAKE MADDOX

SPEED RECEIVER

ILLUSTRATED BY SEAN TIFFANY

text by Eric Stevens

STONE ARCH BOOKS
a capstone imprint

Jake Maddox Books are published by Stone Arch Books
A Capstone Imprint
1710 Roe Crest Drive
North Mankato, Minnesota 56003
www.capstonepub.com

Library of Congress Cataloging-in-Publication Data
Maddox, Jake.
  Speed receiver / by Jake Maddox ; text by Eric Stevens ; illustrated by Sean
Tiffany.
    p. cm. -- (Impact books: a Jake Maddox sports story)
  ISBN 978-1-4342-1636-6 (library binding), 978-1-4342-2780-5 (paperback)
  [1. Football--Fiction.] I. Stevens, Eric, 1974- II. Tiffany, Sean, ill. III. Title.
  PZ7.M25643Sov 2010
  [Fic]--dc22
                                    2010006273

Art Director: Kay Fraser
Graphic Designer: Hilary Wacholz
Production Specialist: Michelle Biedscheid

Photo Credits: ShutterStock/Mike Flippo (p. 2, 3, 4, 5)

TABLE OF CONTENTS

WILDCATS FOOTBALL

SEPT. 8 VS. HORTONVILLE HUSKIES

SEPT. 15 VS. _____

_____ CYCLONES

_____ VS. WHEATON WHALES

29 VS. LYNNES_____

____ VS. BLOOMFI_____

____ VS. EASTLAK_____

WHEATON_____

HORTONV_____

NNESBUR_____

LOOMFIE_____

ANDREW, LOGAN, COACH FRENCH, NOAH, CARLOS

CHAPTER 1

ALL-STAR

The roar of the crowd was deafening. They screamed and cheered, "Andrew! Andrew! Andrew!"

Andrew Tucker smiled through the cage of his helmet. He had scored the winning touchdown of his most important game ever. The fans snapped photos as he danced in the end zone. They all knew someday he'd be the most famous wide receiver in the country.

Scouts from every college and half of the pro teams in the country were watching too. They took notes and shot video footage. Some of them spoke excitedly on cell phones, no doubt telling their team owners or school presidents they had to get this great, young player, quick.

Someone tapped Andrew on the shoulder and he turned. The sun was behind his dad's head, and Andrew squinted.

"Are you listening to me, Andrew?" his dad said.

"Huh?" Andrew replied.

Dad laughed. "I think that you've been daydreaming again," he said. "What are you thinking about this time?"

Andrew sighed. "Same as ever," he said.

The truth was, Andrew wasn't an all-star wide receiver. He played for the junior high football team, and he even got to start most games. But he was lucky if he made one reception per game and one touchdown per season.

The real all-star was Andrew's brother, Marcus. Andrew and his dad were at the Westfield High School Wildcats game right now, and Andrew was dreaming that he was as great as his brother.

Marcus was the one with college and pro scouts watching him. Marcus was the one with adoring fans.

Marcus was the one who had just scored the game-winning touchdown . . . again. It was Marcus's tenth touchdown of the season, and it was only the third game.

Dad stood up from the bleacher. "Another great game for the Wildcats," he said. "I'll get the car. You get your brother."

When Dad had walked off, Andrew got up and headed toward the Wildcats bench. It was crowded with people celebrating and shaking Marcus's hand.

Marcus had fans of all ages. There were other high school guys, some high school girls, plenty of team parents, and even some of the very old men who hung out at the hardware store. Andrew knew some of those men had played on the Westfield Wildcats fifty or sixty years ago.

"Hey, Marcus," Andrew called out. "Come on, bro." He got up on his toes to see over the crowd surrounding his brother. "We have to go."

Marcus shook a few more hands and even signed some little kid's jersey. "Okay, little bro," he said. "Give me a minute."

Andrew stepped back from the crowd and sat on the bench. After a few more minutes, the people went away, and Marcus stood in front of Andrew.

"Ready?" Marcus asked, smiling.

Andrew slowly got to his feet, his shoulders sagging, and said, "Let's go."

The two brothers walked toward Dad's car. Marcus put an arm around his brother's shoulder. "What's wrong?" he asked.

Andrew didn't know what to say. He couldn't admit he was jealous of his brother or that he wanted to be as great on the field as Marcus was.

Just then, Dad honked the horn. The two brothers rounded the school and spotted the family car.

"Race ya!" Marcus said. Even though he had his shoulder pads under one arm and his helmet in one hand, he took off like a shot.

Andrew didn't even try to keep up. "That's why I'm down," he muttered, even though Marcus couldn't hear him. "You're fast, like a wide receiver should be. And I'm not."

CHAPTER 2

RUNNING PLAYS

The Westfield Middle School Wildcats practiced every day after school. Andrew usually looked forward to practice, but on Monday afternoon, he was still feeling down.

"Look alive out there, Andrew," Coach French called out.

"Sorry, Coach," Andrew yelled back. He sighed. He couldn't get himself motivated.

After a few laps on the track, the team

had been running the same old plays over and over. Only one was a long passing play, so Andrew was pretty bored.

The quarterback, Carlos Suarez, counted off. "Hut, hut," he shouted. "Two, two, hut!"

The snap was good. Carlos drew back into the pocket. Andrew went up the right line and then cut across. But play two wasn't a passing play. Andrew's job would be to fake out one defender and then block for the running.

Sure enough, Carlos handed off the ball to Noah Frank, a second-string running back. Then, since this was only a drill, the coach blew the whistle to stop the play. Andrew took a deep breath and headed back to the line.

"Nice job, guys," the coach said. "Andrew, I want to see a little more speed out there. Carlos might decide to look for you if the defensive line is too strong."

"Can we work on my speed, Coach?" Andrew replied. "Do some running drills, maybe?"

Coach French shook his head. "Sorry, Andrew," the coach said. "Our season starts in two days, and we need to get these plays down if we have any chance of running them cleanly."

"How am I going to improve my speed if we only ever practice plays?" Andrew asked. "I mean, it's just drills, so everyone is moving in slow motion, practically. Did you see Noah take that handoff? I think my great-grandma could move faster, and she's ninety-eight!"

A few guys laughed, but Noah looked at his feet. He wasn't the best running back on the team, but he loved the game. Andrew felt bad right away.

"That's enough from you, Andrew," Coach French said, frowning. "One more comment like that, and your speed won't matter. You'll be benched for the rest of the season. Are we clear?"

"Yeah, yeah," Andrew said. He kicked the dirt in front of him. *The field isn't even any good for football*, he thought. *Too dusty. Can't they even keep the grass alive at this school?*

"Now," the coach went on, "we do sprints every day, and we do warm-up laps and warm-down laps, every practice. It's all we have time for."

He clapped once, then said, "Okay, guys. Enough distractions. Let's try that bootleg Carlos has been working on. Line up!"

The team clapped, then got into formation. Andrew was last in line.

GET
LEGS

"Look at that," Marcus said. He was leaning forward on the ratty basement couch, holding tight to the video game controller. His mouth was hanging open in a smile, and his eyes were glazed over. "Ooh, check this out."

Andrew leaned back in the corner of the couch. He watched the TV screen as Marcus tried to beat the last team in their new video game, Soccer Championship.

"Goal!" Marcus shouted. He dropped the controller and jumped off the couch. Then he spun to face Andrew. "Who is the champion?"

"Man, sit down," Andrew said. "It's just a video game."

"Ha," Marcus said. "You're just jealous." But he dropped back down to the couch and flipped off the game.

"Yeah, I am jealous," Andrew admitted, "but not of that dumb soccer game. I'm jealous because I'm too slow on the football field."

"What?" Marcus said. "Who told you that?"

"No one has to tell me," Andrew said. "I know it because I see you out there, like a bolt of lightning. I can't do that."

"Does Coach French work on speed with you?" Marcus asked.

"Not really," Andrew replied. "We spend most of the time going over plays, until everyone has them memorized."

Marcus nodded. He said, "The coach's top priority is to build a winning team. He can't focus all his time and energy on just one player. He's not trying to make stars of you kids. Just football players."

Andrew sighed.

"Don't feel bad," Marcus added. He slapped his brother on the knee. "Remember, it's you that needs to make sure you're the best receiver you can be. It's true for you, and for me, and for every great receiver ever, at every level of the game."

Andrew shook his head. "At least the high school coach helps you with speed drills," he said.

"Yeah," Marcus said, shrugging. "I got some help along the way, no doubt. But it's my legs that take me down the field like a rocket, you know?"

He got up and struck a pose like the Heisman Trophy, and then laughed.

"I don't have your legs," Andrew said. "I have mine."

"That's not what I mean," Marcus said. "It's not just about legs, man."

"So what do you mean?" Andrew asked.

But Marcus just shook his head. "Let's get upstairs," he said, then sniffed the air. "I think dinner's ready."

CHAPTER 4

GETTING IT

The next morning, Andrew sat at the table eating cereal. He took a sip of orange juice.

"Hey, little brother," Marcus said, walking into the room. Andrew smiled, then ate another bite of cereal.

"So," Marcus said, "have you thought about what I said yesterday, before supper?" He grabbed his sneakers from the closet and slipped them on.

"I guess," Andrew said. "But it didn't make any sense. Your legs take you down the field. Duh. And mine take me down the field too, only way more slowly."

Marcus got down on one knee to tie his sneaker. "That's true," he said. Then he switched knees to tie the other sneaker.

"What does that have to do with Coach French?" Andrew asked. He pushed his bowl of cereal away from him and finished the juice. "He still won't let us run speed drills, so I won't be getting any faster."

"Nope," Marcus said, "not just by going to practice. You're probably right."

Marcus stood up and grabbed his backpack from the front closet. He dug around and found his headphones.

"So what's your advice?" Andrew asked.

"Look at it this way," Marcus said. He pulled open the door and looked back at his brother. "How are you getting to school today?"

Andrew shrugged. "Same as always," he said. "The bus. Why?"

Marcus smirked and raised his eyebrows. Then he slipped on his earphones and jogged out the door and down the sidewalk.

Andrew smiled. *I get it*, he thought.

CHAPTER 5

LONG PRACTICE

At practice that afternoon, the team ran two laps together and did some wind sprints. After that, Andrew mostly ran up the field and cut one way or the other. Carlos threw passes to him exactly twice.

"I don't know why I bother washing my jersey," Andrew said after practice. He was walking back to the locker room with his teammate and friend Logan, a linebacker. "I never even break a sweat."

Logan chuckled. "At least we have all the plays down, right?" he said. "The defensive line is really playing great. And the offense looked pretty good today too."

In the locker room, Andrew peeled off his pads and his jersey, but he left on his football pants and sneakers. He shut his locker with a bang.

"Um, Andrew?" Logan said. He was tying his sneakers, dressed in jeans and a nice shirt. "Forgetting something?"

"What do you mean?" Andrew asked.

"I mean you're still wearing half your uniform," Logan said. "Are you going to ride the bus like that?"

Andrew shook his head. "I'm not going to ride the bus at all," he said. "For me, practice isn't over yet."

He saluted Logan and headed outside.

The air was already cooling off after the warm fall day. The sun was setting behind Andrew as he jogged quickly along South Street toward his neighborhood.

"I can do this," he said to himself between breaths. "If this is what it takes to be great, then I'm up for the challenge."

At the corner of Ninth Street, he jogged in place for a minute. His backpack bounced on his shoulders as he waited for the light to change. When it finally did, he jogged on.

Soon, he spotted his house at the end of a long block and started sprinting.

When Andrew stepped through the front door, he checked the clock. 6:45.

"Not too bad," he said, short of breath.

His dad stepped out of the kitchen. "'Not too bad?'" he asked angrily. "Where have you been?"

Andrew tried to catch his breath. "I jogged," he said. "I jogged home. I thought it —"

"You are home an hour later than normal, Andrew!" his dad said, interrupting him. "When I agreed to let you join the football team, you promised to be home for dinner every night and to do your homework the minute you got home."

"I know, Dad, but —" Andrew started, but his dad cut him off again.

"Now you've missed dinner, and your homework still isn't done," Dad said.

Andrew kneeled down to take off his sneakers. "I'm sorry," he said quietly.

Dad nodded. "Okay. Now get changed and washed up," he said. "Then eat dinner. It's cold."

With that, Dad stepped back into the kitchen. Andrew heard his father's chair scrape the floor as Dad sat down to finish his supper.

Andrew put his football sneakers in the front closet and peeked into the kitchen. Dad had his back to him. Marcus was quietly enjoying his spaghetti. He looked up and saw Andrew.

Andrew glared at him. Then he mouthed, "Thanks a lot."

Marcus shrugged. "Not my fault," he mouthed back.

Andrew shook his head and went upstairs to clean up.

CHAPTER 6

LATE TO BED

By the time Andrew got done showering, eating, and doing all his homework, it was late. With a big yawn, he pushed back his chair and stretched his arms and back.

There was a knock at the door.

"Come in," Andrew said.

His dad opened the door. "Is your homework done?" he asked. He had calmed down quite a bit.

"Yeah," Andrew said. "Just finished. I didn't realize how tough that math assignment was going to be. I think I went through ten pencils."

Dad laughed and sat down on the bed. "I'm sorry for getting so angry," Dad said. "But first of all, you need to let me know when you'll be late for supper."

"I know," Andrew said. "I should have called."

Dad nodded. "Second, if your homework is tough, we need to work on it," he said. "And that means you come straight home after practice so we can do that."

Andrew picked at the corner of his math textbook.

"What are you not saying, son?" Dad asked.

Andrew pushed the book away and faced his father. "I need to work on my speed, Dad," Andrew said. "Marcus jogged to and from school every day. He worked hard to get fast so he could be a great receiver. I want to do the same thing."

Dad smiled. "I'm glad you look up to your brother," he said. "He's a hard worker and a great athlete. I'm glad that you want to do the hard work to be great at football."

Andrew glanced at the wall. It was covered with posters of great receivers: Jerry Rice, Randy Moss, Steve Largent.

"But you're young, Andrew," Dad went on. "You need to focus on academics, not athletics. If you can do both, like your brother, that's great. But if it comes down to a conflict between the two, you already know what I'm going to decide."

Dad got up and headed to the door. He glanced at his watch.

"Now, it's late," he said. "You need to get some sleep."

"Especially if I plan to get up early to jog to school tomorrow," Andrew said.

Dad laughed. "That's right," he said. "Good night."

Andrew leaned back in his chair after his dad left the room. He knew he couldn't change his dad's mind. If Andrew wanted to have time to practice and get his speed up, he'd have to find a way to get every bit of homework done too.

CHAPTER 7

EARLY TO RISE

When Andrew's father stepped into the kitchen the next morning, Andrew was tying his sneakers. "What are you doing up?" Dad asked. "It's not even seven."

Andrew glanced up at the hall clock. "Wow," he said. "I'm doing pretty well. See you later, Dad."

"Wait a minute!" Dad replied as Andrew opened the front door. "Why are you leaving so early?"

"I'm going to jog to school," Andrew said. "And there's no way this run will get in the way of my schoolwork, since normally I'd still be sleeping."

Dad scratched his beard and yawned. "I'd like to be sleeping myself," he said. "But at least have some breakfast. You can't run hungry."

"I already ate," Andrew said, stepping outside. "Bye, Dad!"

And with that, he took off running.

* * *

At lunch that day, Andrew leaned on his elbows and stared at the pile of ravioli on his plate.

"Hey, Andrew," Logan said from the across the table. He glanced at Carlos and laughed. "Andrew."

Andrew didn't reply. His eyes felt heavy. He was hungry, but he couldn't bring himself to fork a ravioli and pop it into his mouth.

Suddenly he felt an elbow in his ribs and jumped.

"Hey!" he said. "What was that for?"

Carlos laughed. "Just wanted to make sure you were alive over there," he said.

"Really, Andrew," Logan added with a chuckle. "Were you up all night or something? You look like you're about to pass out."

"Oh, I got up extra early today," Andrew replied. "And I guess I went to bed pretty late last night, too. I jogged home after practice yesterday. And this morning I got up early to jog to school."

"Why?" Carlos asked.

Andrew shrugged. "If Coach French isn't going to give me time at practice to get my speed up, then I have to do it myself," he said. "That's what Marcus says."

Carlos shrugged. "Sounds okay to me," he said. "I wouldn't mind having a wide receiver as good as Marcus to throw to. I hope it works."

"Thanks," Andrew replied. He speared a ravioli and ate it.

"Sure," Carlos said. "But I hope your new schedule isn't making you too tired. After all, today is game day."

Andrew dropped his plastic fork. "Oh no," he said. "I'm exhausted, and I forgot the game is this afternoon!"

CHAPTER 8

EXHAUSTED

Andrew's afternoon didn't go well. At one point during government class, Logan had to kick his foot to wake him up. The teacher nearly caught him sleeping.

"You're never going to make it through the whole game," Logan said as the two boys got changed into their uniforms after school. "Maybe you should tell the coach you're sick. You can go home and get some sleep."

Andrew stifled a yawn. "No way," he said. "I haven't been running and working on my speed just to go home and sleep."

Logan shrugged. "Okay," he said. "But I have a feeling you won't be moving too fast out there today."

Logan slammed his locker shut and headed out to the field. Andrew grabbed his helmet and sat on the bench.

"I have to get some energy," he said to himself. "I can't let one bad night's sleep ruin the game for me."

Andrew nodded to himself and closed his locker. "I can do this," he said. Then he headed out to the field.

As soon as he started running, Andrew knew he was more tired than he'd thought. The first quarter was really tiring.

During the second quarter, Carlos called a passing play. Andrew would have to sprint about fifteen yards off the line, then cut to the right.

"Hut, hut, hike!" Carlos called, and the center snapped the ball. Carlos drew back, and Andrew took off from the line.

Carlos released the ball perfectly, but when Andrew cut to the right he lost his footing and slipped. The defender, who had kept up with Andrew easily, snatched the ball from the air.

"Interception!" Carlos called out.

The other team's player ran along the sideline for ten yards before being forced out of bounds.

"Look alive out there, Andrew!" Coach French called from the sidelines.

Andrew pulled off his helmet and headed to the bench with the rest of the offense. "Sorry, Coach," Andrew said. He dropped onto the bench.

Carlos stood in front of him. "So much for having a receiver as good as Marcus," Carlos said. "That was awful."

Andrew glared up at him. Carlos just shook his head and walked off.

At halftime, Andrew headed to the locker room. Marcus was waiting for him. Andrew's brother grabbed his arm. "Just a second, little brother," Marcus said. "I want to talk to you."

"What?" Andrew said. "I can't stand around out here. I'm not exactly popular on the team right now. If I miss the halftime huddle, I'll probably get expelled from school."

"I just need a minute," Marcus said. "You look pretty tired out there."

"Yeah," Andrew said. "I got up early."

"Dad told me," Marcus said. "He said you jogged to school today, too. Good for you."

Andrew shrugged.

"But you're making the same mistake I made at first," Marcus said. "It took me weeks to figure it out, so I'll let you in on my secret. Schedule."

"Schedule?" Andrew repeated.

"Simple, really," Marcus said. "But I failed a math test and got a D in Spanish before I figured it out. Dad was threatening to pull me off the football team."

"What did you do?" Andrew asked.

"I looked at my whole day," Marcus said. "I made choices. For example, I used to have lunch with some friends of mine. We'd take the whole half hour, goof off, sometimes start trouble in the cafeteria."

"Yeah," Andrew said, smiling. "That's what Logan and Carlos and I do."

"But I bet you get some homework in the morning, right?" Marcus asked.

"Sure," Andrew said. "I always do."

"You could have all that homework done by now if you worked while you ate, instead of goofing off," Marcus explained.

"I see what you mean," Andrew said.

Marcus patted him on the back. "Okay. Now get into that halftime meeting before they send you off to play for the other team," he said.

CHAPTER 9

TIMING

That night, after the game and after he'd done his homework, Andrew looked over his schedule.

The next game was a week away. If he did his morning homework during lunch, he'd have extra time to run after school. If he skipped playing Championship Soccer with his brother some nights, he could get to bed early and be up in time for a morning run, too.

That week, Andrew was very busy. The morning after the game, he woke up early and ran sprints in the park near his house. He even had time to shower and catch the bus afterward.

At lunch, he spotted Logan and Carlos at their usual table, but he headed off to a quiet corner with his tray of food.

Andrew pulled out his books and started his math homework. After a few minutes, he realized someone was standing behind him. He turned to look.

"Hi, Carlos," Andrew said. "Hi, Logan." His two teammates stood there, smiling at him.

"What are you doing?" Carlos said. "It's lunchtime. You're not supposed to be doing homework now."

"Yeah," Logan said. "What, did you leave your homework for the last minute? Is this due next period or something?"

Andrew shook his head. "Nope," he said. "This is the homework Ms. Finnegan assigned in math today. I'm getting it done now so I can work out tonight."

Carlos and Logan looked at each other. Then Carlos put a hand on Andrew's head. "Hm," he said. "He doesn't have a fever."

"Maybe we should call the nurse anyway," Logan said. "Just to be on the safe side."

"Ha ha," Andrew said without smiling. "You guys are hilarious. Now leave me alone so I can work."

Carlos shook his head. Logan slapped Andrew on the back as they walked away.

That weekend, Andrew had plenty of free time. Normally he'd spend it at the mall with his friends, or playing video games with his brother. Not this weekend, though. He had a game coming up, and he needed to get ready.

"Andrew!" his dad called. "Logan is on the phone. Are you meeting some guys from the team down at the mall today?"

Andrew was at the front door, putting on his sneakers. "No, Dad," he called back. "I'm going running. Tell Logan I'll see him Monday. We can hang out next weekend."

He pulled open the door and flew down the sidewalk toward the track at the park, leaving Dad holding the phone.

CHAPTER 10

WILDCATS VS. LIONS

As busy as he was, Andrew could hardly believe a week had gone by. But it was game day again, and this week, Westfield was facing their rivals, the Lions from Libertyville.

This time, though, Andrew wasn't tired. He was rested and in great shape.

In the first quarter, Andrew stepped up to Carlos before a huddle. "Throw it to me," he said. "I can lose this defender, easy."

Carlos shook his head. "And you can slip on the grass and give him the ball to catch, too, huh?" he said.

"That won't happen today," Andrew said. "Look, call whatever play you want. But keep an eye on me, okay?"

Carlos looked at Andrew for a moment. "Fine," he said. "I'll look for you, but no promises."

The boys joined the huddle. Carlos called an option, and then shouted, "Break!"

The offense formed their line and Carlos called for the snap: "Hut!"

Carlos drew back, and Andrew took off like a shot. He ran out about thirty yards, then cut hard back and to the left sideline. His defender cut too, but not as smoothly.

Andrew was wide open. Carlos was watching, and he drew back quickly and released for the long pass. It flew at Andrew's chest. Andrew closed his hands over the ball and dodged quickly as his defender dove at him.

Andrew turned toward the end zone, but two defenders were on top of him. He went down at the forty.

"Nice!" Carlos called out, clapping and running up to the new line of scrimmage. Andrew jogged to the huddle. His teammates gave him high fives.

"Way to lose that defender, Andrew," Carlos said. "You're starting to look like Marcus out there."

Andrew smiled and got ready for the next play.

* * *

By the fourth quarter, the score was 7-10, Wildcats.

Andrew was playing his best, but passing games were tough. He'd made some nice receptions, but the Wildcats points came from a quarterback sneak and one field goal.

Meanwhile, the Lions' short game was really on that day. With only a few minutes left in the fourth quarter, their running back took a surprise hand-off. He ran up the sideline for forty yards and a touchdown. After the extra point kick, the score was 14-10, Lions.

"All right, guys," Carlos said in the huddle after the kick-off. "We need to score, fast."

"There's less than one minute on the clock," one of the Wildcats linemen said. "This game is over."

"Nice attitude," Carlos replied, shaking his head. He looked at Andrew. "Can you lose that defender again?"

"Sure," Andrew replied. "Just say when."

"Now," Carlos said. "I want you to go as long as I can throw. Go out to their forty and cut to the right. I'll find you. Okay?"

Everyone nodded. "Good," Carlos said. He clapped and said, "Break!"

At the line, Andrew's heart was racing. He thought about the last week and how hard he'd worked. He'd missed a couple of movies, and Marcus was now much better at Championship Soccer than he was.

But none of that mattered now. What mattered was the effort and the game.

"Hut," Carlos called. "Hut!"

The center snapped the ball, and Andrew took off. He had five yards on his defender right away.

Andrew pumped his arms at his side. He was at the Lions' forty in no time, and he faked to the left, then turned right. He looked up just as Carlos released the pass.

Andrew's defender stumbled a bit when Andrew cut. By the time he recovered, the ball was at Andrew's open hands.

He caught the pass perfectly and took a sharp left toward the end zone. The field was wide open, from the forty to the one. He was home free. And Andrew ran, as fast as he could.

Andrew's legs seemed to move on their own. He imagined he was on his own street, running over the broken sidewalk, past his neighbors' houses and the blue mailbox on the corner.

He smiled, and then kicked up his speed even more.

"Touchdown!" the referee called out, throwing up his arms.

Andrew stopped on the far side of the end zone and threw down the football. Then he pulled off his helmet and looked up at the clock. Only two seconds remained.

Carlos came sprinting up the field. "Now it's over," he shouted. The whole offense was right behind him. They picked Andrew up and carried him to the bench.

Coach French and Andrew's brother were there, cheering like crazy.

"Great reception, little brother," Marcus said. "I guess the schedule is working."

"You know it," Andrew said.

Coach French said, "If you keep up this hard work, I have a feeling you'll be up against your brother in the pro draft before you know it."

Marcus and Andrew laughed.

"I don't know, Coach," Andrew said. "I think I'll keep making academics a priority for now."

The coach nodded. "Good idea," he said.

"Besides," Marcus added, "I'm sure Andrew and I will get a chance to face each other when we're both in the pros."

THE AUTHOR
ERIC STEVENS

15

ERIC STEVENS LIVES IN ST. PAUL, MINNESOTA WITH HIS WIFE, DOG, AND SON. HE IS STUDYING TO BECOME A TEACHER. SOME OF HIS FAVORITE THINGS INCLUDE PIZZA AND VIDEO GAMES. SOME OF HIS LEAST FAVORITE THINGS INCLUDE OLIVES AND SHOVELING SNOW.

WHEN SEAN TIFFANY WAS GROWING UP, HE LIVED ON A SMALL ISLAND OFF THE COAST OF MAINE. EVERY DAY UNTIL HE GRADUATED FROM HIGH SCHOOL, HE HAD TO TAKE A BOAT TO GET TO SCHOOL! SEAN HAS A PET CACTUS NAMED JIM.

24

THE ILLUSTRATOR
SEAN TIFFANY

GLOSSARY

academics (ak-uh-DEM-iks)—to do with study and learning

conflict (KON-flict)—a disagreement

drills (DRILZ)—ways to learn things by repeating actions over and over

exhausted (eg-ZAWST-id)—very tired

focus (FOH-kuhss)—concentration or attention

improve (im-PROOV)—to get better

motivated (MOH-tuh-vate-id)—feeling excited to do something

priority (prye-OR-uh-tee)—something that is more important than something else

schedule (SKEJ-ool)—how a day is planned

second-string (SEK-uhnd STRING)—backup

tough (TUFF)—difficult

DISCUSSION QUESTIONS

1. If you were Andrew, what things in this book would you have done differently?

2. Did Marcus give his brother good advice? Why or why not?

3. How do you balance all of the different things you need to do? Talk about it.

WRITING PROMPTS

1. Pretend that you're Andrew's big brother. Write him a letter explaining how he can improve his skills.

2. Write about an older sibling, cousin, or friend who inspires you.

3. What do you think happens when this book ends? Write a chapter that continues the story.

MORE ABOUT WIDE RECEIVERS

In this book, Andrew Tucker is a wide receiver for the Westfield Wildcats. Check out these quick facts about wide receivers.

- Wide receivers are key members of the offense in a football team.

- To be great players, wide receivers must be able to catch and throw well, and run fast. Being able to run fast can enable a wide receiver to get away from the other team's defense in order to catch a pass, or to block the running back.

- Wide receivers must move quickly to help prevent interceptions when passes go wrong.

- Some famous wide receivers include Randy Moss, Terrell Owens, Marvin Harrison, Chad Johnson, Lynn Swann, and Chris Carter.

THE WILDCATS